For Ily, Moon, and Gabe

First Aladdin Books edition 1993. Copyright © 1990 by Catherine Stock. All rights reserved. No part of this book may be reproduced or transmitted in any form or by any means, electronic or mechanical, including photocopying, recording, or by any information storage and retrieval system, without permission in writing from the Publisher. Aladdin Books, Macmillan Publishing Company, 866 Third Avenue, New York, NY 10022. Maxwell Macmillan Canada, Inc., 1200 Eglinton Avenue East, Suite 200, Don Mills, Ontario M3C 3N1. Macmillan Publishing Company is part of the Maxwell Communication Group of Companies. Printed in Hong Kong by South China Printing Company (1988) Ltd.
10 9 8 7 6 5 4 3 2

The text of this book is set in 20 point Palatino. The illustrations are rendered in watercolor. A hardcover edition of *Thanksgiving Treat* is available from Bradbury Press, an affiliate of Macmillan, Inc.

Library of Congress Cataloging–in–Publication Data
Stock, Catherine.
    Thanksgiving treat / by Catherine Stock. —1st Aladdin Books ed.
        p.   cm.
    Summary: There seems to be no place for the smallest child in a family's busy preparations for Thanksgiving, until Grandpa steps in and they perform a vital task everyone else has forgotten.
    ISBN 0-689-71726-1
    [1. Thanksgiving Day—Fiction.]   I. Title.
PZ7.S8635Th 1993
[E]—dc20   92-43690

Thanksgiving Treat

BY CATHERINE STOCK

ALADDIN BOOKS
Macmillan Publishing Company   *New York*
Maxwell Macmillan Canada   *Toronto*
Maxwell Macmillan International
New York   Oxford   Singapore   Sydney

I am at Grandma and Grandpa's
house. It's Thanksgiving and
everybody is here—my mother
and father and brother and sister
and aunts and uncles and all my
cousins. The house is full.

The house is busy. Grandma and Mommy are stuffing the turkey.

"Can I help you?" I ask.

"Not now, sweetie," says Mommy.

"Careful, the oven is hot," warns Grandma. "See if you can help your sister."

My sister, Marianne, and the
other girls are peeling potatoes
and scraping carrots.

"Can I help you?" I ask.

"You're too little. You'll scrape
your fingers," they say.

Aunt Sally is making pumpkin
pies and cranberry sauce with
my other aunts.

"Careful, honey. You nearly
knocked over the cinnamon. Go
see if you can help the boys,"
she says.

My cousins are shucking corn
on the veranda.

"We can do this," they say.
"You can go and play outside."

Daddy and Uncle Pete are
chopping firewood.

"Keep back," calls Daddy.
"There are splinters flying
about."

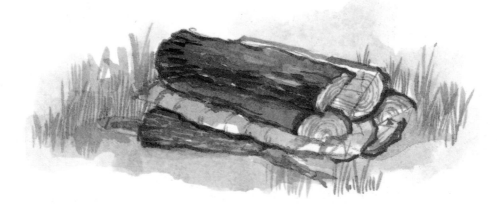

I go and sit on the swing.
Everybody is busy. Everybody is
having a good time. Everybody
except me.

"What's up, champ?" It's
Grandpa. "Got a minute?"

"Sure." I run over to Grandpa.

We go out the gate and down
the muddy road.
"Where are we going, Grandpa?"
"You'll see."

At the end of the apple orchard
is a big tree.

"Chestnuts," says Grandpa.
"I'll knock them down with my
stick if you pick them up and
put them in this basket."

Soon the basket is full.
    We sniff the cool evening air
as we walk home. Someone has
lit a wood fire.

"Chestnuts!" everyone cries when
we come in. "You found some
chestnuts to roast in the fire!"

Grandma brings a bowl of sweet
butter and the salt shaker.

Grandpa splits the chestnuts
with his pocketknife and we
poke them into the fire.

Mmm, they are good!